Awake:
Unsleeping Beauty

By
Louisa Bacio

Copyright © 2016 by Louisa Bacio
ISBN: 978-1-68361-081-6
Cover art by Tibbs Designs

Published by Decadent Publishing Company, LLC
Look for us online at:
www.decadentpublishing.com

Dedication

Special thanks to the women who support me: Joanne Best for beta reading this tale, Anastasia Vitsky who asked many times when it was going to be done, and Kate Richards for her continued support.

Finally, to the ladies of Short in Six. Much love!

As bright as a flash of lightning streaking across a storm-darkened night, the story unfurls.

Sometimes rules are meant to be broken, and new traditions forged. This tale follows two princesses— one who never wakes and another who rarely sleeps. Somehow, they must overcome the obstacles in order to find happiness.

Chapter One

O nce more, rough, persistent lips pressed against hers. Briar Rose fought against the wet, slimy tongue as it tried to force into her mouth. She couldn't move and couldn't protect herself. She was trapped within the invisible bonds of a sleep-like state. A curse suspended her in sleep, and yet she remained aware of her surroundings and the comings and goings of others.

She was tired of men kissing her without her consent. Who cared if they were princes or knights or ogres? No one had any idea what their breath smelled like or tasted like at the end of a grand adventure or the way their sweaty hair brushed her face as she lay powerless to swat it away. No matter the fairy-tale lore, kisses from any of them had failed to wake her. None of them so far had possessed the power to rescue her and claim the throne.

Meeeeoooow! Hisss! At least she had one comfort. Puss, her dedicated feline, eventually chased off the suitors when their kisses failed to wake her.

"Get off me, psycho cat!" a man cursed. "She's not worth it anyway, lying there like a piece of meat."

The latest savior shrieked, and Puss howled. She imagined the feisty cat landing atop a messy head of hair and digging its claws in.

Raaaaoooor!

"Awww! I didn't mean it." *Thud.* The latest suitor must have stumbled to the floor. Footsteps clunked down the hall, and a door slammed.

Still, she lay there. Paralyzed. The bed dipped as

Puss returned to Rose's side, running his body under her hand, as if she were petting him. If she could cry, she would have at his caring and gentle nature. His gentle purring sent a pleasant hum through her body as he curled against the side of her head, and she escaped into her dreams, imagining the day she'd find release.

***

Princess Penelope flounced her dark curls over the fluffy down pillow and willed herself to sleep. She shifted against the sapphire satin sheets, shivering at the caress of the fabric against her bare body. She had no idea how to sleep suffocated in chiffon and buried in a tidal wave of pillows. Her father must have possessed a handbook for how princesses should sleep because this bed was not her choice and it certainly wasn't doing her any favors. She punched down the billowing layers of comforters, causing a windstorm of soft white feathers to escape and rain upon her.

"Ah-choo! Awwww-choo!" she brushed a persistent offender from her nose. Being allergic to down didn't help either. Try telling that to the king, her father. He'd hear none of it.

Hour after hour, she lay in bed, staring at the undulating fabric dangling from the canopy. Hardness—like the pointiest rock in the world—poked right below her shoulder blade. She turned and flopped, but the sharpness couldn't be escaped and it dug into the corner of her hip.

Beneath her left thigh, a seam increased its pressure, cutting into her tender flesh. She flipped.

From this position she could see out her bedchamber's window. A cool breeze carried in the scent of honeysuckle. Her nose itched, and she scrunched it up, trying not to think about the need to sneeze.

"Ahhhh-chooo."

She shook her head, clearing the tingling, and mentally listed all the tasks tomorrow held. Oh, she might have everyday duties such as choosing the menu for the end-of-the-season banquet or instructing the chambermaids about the correct manner in which to arrange the linen cupboards, but, still, someone had to run the palace, and that someone ultimately was her.

There was no older brother, no prince to take over the throne. As the eldest, Penelope held all the responsibilities but none of the respect.

What time was it? Certainly she'd been lying there, tangled up in her sweaty sheets for hours. And with that thought, she became aware of the ticking of a clock in the otherwise quiet room.

Tick. Tick. Tick. Ticktickticktick.

"For crying out loud," she announced to the room at large. "What's it going to take for me to fall asleep?"

That afternoon, she'd overheard the king talking to his advisers about a princess cursed with perpetual sleep locked in a hidden castle. Penelope lay awake, mind racing with thoughts about the dangers and adventure lying beyond the castle's walls.

"Only a prince can save Briar Rose," her father had said.

Why? Penelope could do anything her younger brothers could and then some. She knew her father wished they'd been born first, and her later. He needed to marry her, the oldest, off and then wait for them to grow old enough to do anything. At twelve and fourteen, they were still mastering the art of riding a horse, forget about running the castle or taking adventures to far-off lands.

What would the princess look like? She was probably fair, with long, blonde curly hair, and porcelain skin—nothing like Penelope's own unruly dark hair and nose heavily freckled from too much sun. Penelope imagined the other princess's lips were soft as rose petals. She probably resembled her name in more than one way. As she fantasized, she slipped a hand beneath her robe and fingered her tender nether lips, dipping her middle finger into her wetness and stroking the bud of pleasure.

Suppressing a moan, she bit her lower lip and increased the friction. Penelope admired the swell of the woman's breasts, and the way the dress flowed over Briar Rose's thighs. If Penelope were to slip her head under the covers and nibble on Briar's Rose's inner thigh, would she wake? If she delved her tongue into the cleft between her legs.... Ah, she shivered at the mere idea.

All the ladies at the balls went on and on about which prince was available, who possessed the biggest—ahem—carriage, and who had the best-endowed dowry. But Penelope had never felt a flutter in her heart or a pulse in her pussy at the thought of a strong, handsome man. She sought adventure of another sort.

No prince had ever captured Penelope's interest. Heat didn't flare between her legs when a dashing, muscled man requested her hand in a dance. And, yet, alas, she fantasized about an imaginary woman locked away, completely helpless. The princess would not be able to shun Penelope's advances. She wouldn't laugh at her hidden desires.

Maybe, she'd even be thankful to be rescued. Maybe she'd place a soft kiss against Penelope's lips and press the soft curves of her body against Penelope.

Yes, she might be thankful.

Penelope had never been with a man, so she had no experience with the opposite sex. But she knew what felt good. As she touched herself, her muscles pulled taut, and she dangled on the precipice of something great. She knew not what, yet she knew she approached something wonderful. Her lashes fluttered against her cheekbones, and her hips arched in anticipation.

What would it feel like to have Briar Rose's supple fingers stroking her, pushing her to that elusive edge, and then over? She climbed higher, and higher and—

"Awwwe-choo!" *Damn.* She turned over onto her back, and whatever boulder lay beneath her mattresses probed her in the ass. She fought to ignore the pain and a sudden cramp in her arm. She switched hands, trying not to lose the momentum.

What goes up, must come down, or so the saying goes, but no matter how high she went, she never transferred over to the other side. She never came, never had. Oh, she'd heard the word, and the whispers. The stable boys, in particular, liked to gossip about bodily urges and functions, but with Penelope...nothing.

Frustrated, she groaned and fluffed her pillows,

totally giving up on any chance of finishing. She lay in her frilly canopy bed, lost among a sea of bedding, and prayed she was not doomed to stay awake— forever.

Obviously, she'd slept some time during the night. Even as an insomniac, she had to in order to survive. But never enough. Night after night, she lay awake, counting sheep, trying with all her might, and yet still nothing worked.

She fantasized about the woman of her dreams. As a princess who couldn't sleep, one who did nothing but dream seemed to be the perfect case of opposites attract. Before she could start her quest, Penelope needed to escape the kingdom. When the time came, she'd figure out how to rescue Briar Rose. First, she needed to wake her.

***

At breakfast, Penelope's head dipped, and sleep weighed down her eyelids. The bowl of oatmeal before her congealed, and as she lifted the spoon, it felt like solid gold rather than gold-plated.

"Another bad night, Pea?" Russell, the older of her brothers, asked. "You look like something the giants dragged in."

After taking a bite of his blueberry scone, Russell brushed the crumbs off the cream linen tablecloth and onto the floor. During meals, Buttercup, the royal pet Corgi, hung out under the table, knowing discards would be coming his way.

At the question, their father studied her before tsking. "How are you ever going to win the hand of a prince, if you can't even make yourself presentable?"

"Oh, Dad." She reached over and patted the back of his hand. "You know I don't want to get married. Whoever would take care of you?"

The king harrumphed. The rest of her siblings at the table became extra intrigued with their meals.

"Your mother, the kingdom rest her soul, would not want you to waste your life away caring for me and your kin. We both wanted more for you, and from you."

Tears welled in her eyes. They rarely spoke of her mother, who had died giving birth to her baby sister Gwennie five years before. The king had never remarried, and more often than not, Penelope helped with her siblings, whether needed or not. With a castle full of servants, none of the children wanted for anything—except the love of a mother. And that's where Penelope stepped in.

"My time will come." She drew from the list of responses she'd developed. She reached for the silver teapot and poured herself another cup, adding two lumps of sugar.

"Tell her, Dad," Russell said.

A smattering of unease crept along Penelope's spine, and traveled up. "Tell me what?" she couldn't help but ask.

"Well, there's something I've been meaning to talk with you about," he started.

As she watched him, the king shifted his gaze away so as not to look at her directly. She knew this was going to be bad.

"In two weeks' time, there will be a ball, and at that dance you'll have to proclaim your choice in a mate." He set the guidelines.

"But, Father...."

He held up a hand. "I've been patient the past few years while I let you get your feet under you, but it's time. You're twenty-three and not getting any younger. You've rejected every prince who's come to the castle, and a few knights, too. Now, you must make a decision, or I will make it for you."

"Maybe it's not a prince she's wanting," her younger brother Jeremy teased.

"Hush now." Russell punched him in the arm. "Leave Pea alone."

"Owwww." Jeremy rubbed his arm, and pouted.

Ahhh, the joys of being the eldest. She waited for her father to say whatever else he needed to say.

"It's already set." Her father placed his hands on the table and finally met her gaze directly. Crinkles of kindness creased the sides of his eyes. "Invitations have been sent out. You have two weeks of freedom, and then you must choose a mate."

Penelope thought of the Princess Briar Rose trapped in the castle, and of her own fate trapped in a marriage she didn't want. Terror lapped at her psyche.

"Fine, two weeks," she said. "But until then, I ask that you'll indulge me in a little adventure."

Chapter Two

Going anywhere alone was forbidden. Just because her life would essentially be taken away in just two weeks shouldn't have made Penelope think this excursion would be any different. The king had relented, allowing her to venture out into the kingdom. If only he knew what she planned.

In the stables, Penelope greeted each horse. The air smelled like dried hay with a sweet undertone of oats and honey. She'd brought an apple in her coat pocket, and stopped before Midnight's stall. The stallion whinnied when he saw her approaching, and she couldn't help smiling. Despite her proven track record, her father didn't like to hear about her riding Midnight. Too big and too male for her—perfect as a stud horse, but too wild as a ride.

She rarely listened to warnings. Nothing good ever came from following orders. By her age, she'd learned the best things came from breaking traditions and more than bending the rules at times.

While her father had forbidden her to do certain things, riding Midnight didn't fall on that list. She knew he'd feel strongly about it if he found out. But he'd never put limitations on her riding him, so she technically wasn't breaking any rules. If it were up to her father, she'd be mounted on a slow, steady old mare. For everyday, such a horse might not be too bad, but for covering long territory, she wanted an equine that moved faster. One with spirit.

As she neared, she removed the apple from her pocket and placed it in the middle of her flattened palm. Midnight didn't need much convincing. As he ate, she rubbed him on his nose and cooed.

"You're a good boy, aren't you?"

Midnight lifted his head, nudging her. Either he wanted more food or he wanted more attention. She couldn't give him either at the moment. After rubbing his nose along the white streak, she kissed him, whispering about the journey to come.

After checking with the stable hands that Midnight would be ready at the appointed time, she returned to the house to finish packing. The castle was eerily quiet as she entered and went up the stairs.

As the excitement of getting ready waned, Penelope questioned her course of action. The laughter of her brothers playing echoed off the walls and pained her heart. In the years since their mother's death, she'd taken on the emotional responsibilities of the family. Guilt plagued her thoughts. Was it fair for her to leave them? What would happen if she didn't return?

As she walked down the hallway, soft sobs reached her ears. Gwennie stepped out of her room, her bottom lip twitching and silent tears slipping across her pink cheeks. She struggled to catch her breath. Without a mama, she'd never had the chance to be a baby and had always kept the "stiff upper lip" the king stressed.

"Oh, honey, come here." Penelope opened her arms.

The mini princess ran into her embrace, and Pea enveloped her. She breathed in the girl's fresh scent. "What's the matter?"

"I-I-I don't want you to go," she said. "Why do you need to go?"

Nothing like seeing the guilt manifest. She guided her little sister to the bed, and patted the spot next to her. "I know it's not easy to understand, but you heard Dad. It'll soon be time for me to marry. As the oldest in the family, it's my responsibility. Once I do, maybe you can live with me."

"Really?" she lightened right away.

I shouldn't make promises I can't keep.

"Maybe. Or maybe I'll still live here. You never know."

Her little sister's bright-blue eyes shone up at her. The afternoon light caught the shimmer of tears and reflected hope. "But why do you have to leave? In the fairy tales, when someone goes on a journey, they never return."

"Oh, that won't be me," she answered right away. "I'll return—victorious!" She lifted her voice at the end, emphasizing her words with more energy than normal.

Still, she pondered her little sister's question. Why did she have to leave indeed? More than anything, Pea had a feeling. A sense she needed to do something. Before hearing about Briar Rose, she'd had a persistent sense of purpose. She'd always felt different—apart—from other girls her age. She'd never been distracted by frilly lace or pink satin. And yet, the thought of Briar Rose trapped and cursed in perpetual sleep compelled her. She needed to see the princess, and maybe do something about her.

How to explain all that to a child?

"As for the 'why,' you know when there's a special something you want? And you can't hold still or stop talking about it until you've got it?"

The munchkin tilted her head and looked past Penelope, as if she focused on a memory. "Yes, like when I want Mama. Like that?"

The longing in her voice struck deep. She'd been thinking a trinket or a new kitty, and Gwennie had taken the conversation to another level. Typical.

Softly, she rocked her sister, stroking her hair and feeling that familial connection bonding them together. "Something like that. Right now, I feel like there's something out there waiting for me to discover it. If I stay here and never try, then I'll never know, right?"

"But, why…?"

"Tell me something you might want me to bring back for you?" Penelope had learned to head her off before she asked even more questions, or, in this case, the same one over and over again.

"How about a flower from the prettiest rosebush you see?"

The request threw Penelope off. She hoped the prettiest rose she would see would be Briar Rose. Would she be able to bring her home?

"What a wonderful idea. Now, how about you help me decide what to pack."

The rest of the evening passed by quickly, until bedtime when she went room to room, kissing each sibling good night. Gwennie ran so hard every day that when she crashed, she zonked out. The boys, on the other hand, always seemed to be able to go and go, until they didn't anymore. She wouldn't miss this last night for anything.

"You're not going to do anything dumb out there, are you?" Russell asked. His brow furrowed as he waited for her answer.

"Define dumb." She ruffled his hair.

With a scowl of discontent, he smoothed it back down again. "Dangerous."

"You better watch out," Penelope teased, "or you'll start sounding like a king."

"Humph. I don't see why I can't come along with you."

Oh no. Everyone was suddenly interested in watching out for Penelope. Since when had events turned?

"I need you to do something for me while I'm gone," Penelope said.

"I'm listening."

"Well, you know how I'm mostly in charge of looking after you guys?"

"Yes...."

"Well, that responsibility now goes to you. You know how Dad is, getting all wrapped up in his duties. Especially now with this ball coming up. Make sure Gwennie and Jeremy follow their studies and wash behind their ears." She ran her fingers through his hair again, and, this time, he sank deeper into the pillow and closed his eyes.

"All right. Just promise me you'll be back soon." His breathing evened out.

"I promise."

Laying a kiss on his forehead, she recited two small internal prayers—one to keep the family safe during her leave, and another to keep her safe during the journey. Now, if only she'd be able to keep all these promises.

Her departure time set for early morning, Penelope once again lay in bed awake. Every time she shut her eyes, an onslaught of intense images and echoing screams took over. During those rare moments when she actually fell asleep, the blackest of night terrors struck. Paralyzed, she'd lie frozen, fear spreading through her body like black oil coating her soul. Gasping for breath, she'd stutter awake and refuse to go back to sleep.

Usually, to hold off the fatigue, she'd try every remedy possible, including magical concoctions by the kingdom's healer supposed to help her stay alert and keep her body running. Some worked not at all, and some not so well. She didn't need to sleep.

Except, some nights, like this one, she wished for sleep to come fast, if only to make the next day come that much faster.

**

Despite being trapped in a dream world, Briar Rose's imagination worked overtime, providing a rich tapestry almost as tangible as, well, real life. Most of the time, her savior stayed in the shadows. She always had a sense someone was coming, but she could never see who. If she was having a normal dream, she'd wake right before the unveiling. Her curse remained. Over and over, the cycle looped, never letting her reach that final moment.

Until now. Everything in the same repeated dream changed.

Outside, birds sang a glorious tune, and Rose vocalized with them. She dug her bare feet into the damp soil and picked up fallen rose petals, rubbing the fragrance between her fingertips.

The sound of horses approaching overshadowed the wildlife, and she ducked behind a huge tree trunk to hide. Her first impression was of a massive horse, black as night. If she'd stood in front of him, she would have only reached mid-chest. His muscular front legs danced after his rider reined him in.

"It's all right boy, it's all right," a melodious woman's voice soothed the beast. He whinnied in return, as if engaging in a conversation with her.

A slender white hand petted the side of the stallion's head. A woman on a horse that big? Impossible. Her parents would never.... At the thought of her mother and father, despair surged through her imaginings. She wanted to touch them, see them, and talk with them again.

"Hello? Is anyone there?" the woman called out. "Did you hear someone singing, Midnight? I swear I just did, but I don't see anyone here."

The horse pranced in a circle and they turned, exploring the enclave. She caught sight of a panted leg. A woman in pants, atop a great steed? It couldn't be. She rode astride. Rose grew even more curious.

"Whoa, there. Steady." The woman swung her other leg over and skillfully dropped to the forest floor.

Briar Rose could see her as though she stood directly in her line of sight. Taller than Rose, with dark, unruly hair drawn back in a leather band. The woman rubbed her hands over her thighs and turned to remove something from the horse's pouch. Leaning forward to catch a better glimpse, Briar fell over and tumbled through the bushes and onto the ground at the traveler's feet.

"Oh," she exclaimed, leaping up and brushing off the fine silk of her pale-pink gown. "Oh, dear. It's ruined."

Remembering the other woman looking on, Briar turned to run.

"Wait, don't go. I'm searching for you."

Those words sank through. "You're what?"

"I think. I mean, you must be Briar Rose, right?"

"How do you know that?" She'd never seen this person before. Her unease surpassed her curiosity. "My mama used to tell me if I think on a problem before I go to sleep then my dreams will show me the answer." She turned in a slow circle, taking in the surroundings. "And I was thinking about you."

"Me?" Briar touched her chest and realized her mouth hung open. "Why should I believe you? Or trust you?"

"Maybe you shouldn't. But from what I've heard, you're trapped in a castle under a magical spell, in need of rescuing. I aim to rescue you."

"Rescue? Me? Do you have any idea how many princes and knights have tried and failed? What makes you think you have any better chance at getting the job done?"

In anger, she strode forward, pointing and ready to poke her "rescuer."

"So tell me, young miss, are you a naughty princess?" the strange woman asked. She blushed. "Those were men. As you can see, I have certain qualities they do not."

As she talked, Briar studied the woman's lips. How soft they appeared as she spoke so boldly. She wondered what they would feel like against hers. So tired of the men's rough and prodding mouths pressing upon hers, she longed for a bit of romance and finessing.

The woman covered her mouth with her hand. "Is something wrong? Do I have something on my face? You keep staring."

"Oh, I'm sorry. I'm just intrigued. You talk with such strength. Where in the world did you find it?"

"Why, we all have it. You only need to believe in yourself."

As she moved forward, Briar's breath caught in her throat. Light streamed through the openings in the branches ahead and streaked across the woman's hair catching strands of gold and ruby. Absolutely stunning.

The woman gazed upon the beginning stages of the rising sun. "It's almost dawn. I must go because the adventure begins." She turned back toward her horse.

"Wait," Briar called out. "Do not leave yet. You know who I am. How will I know you? What is your name?"

"Princess Penelope," she said with a slight smile. "And I'm quite sure you'll be seeing me again. If not in the real world, then this one."

Reality grew fuzzy, and Briar tried to hold onto the image of Penelope for as long as possible. The woman didn't ride off into the sunrise but simply faded from existence into the nothingness normally plaguing Briar's life. Except, now, she had hope.

Chapter Three

Morning brought a renewed sense of anticipation. Sunlight streamed into Penelope's room, and she washed up and dressed in record time. She packed a few items, and ventured downstairs to the kitchen for supplies of the edible variety. Upon seeing her, the cook's eyes grew watery.

"Oh, mistress. Is it really necessary for you to leave?" Kind Matilda dabbed at the corners of her eyes with the edge of her apron, leaving a dusting of flour in its wake.

Over the past two days, Penelope had reassured everyone. Now, with a jumble of nerves trotting in her stomach, she needed some reassurance back, but still she soothed the old cook. "There, there. I'll be back eating your meat pies faster than you know it. Plus, I hear you have a big ball to get ready for."

"We will all miss you, but I'm sure your future will be a good one," Matilda said. "Your father....You know he means well." She turned back toward the stove, stirring a big, steaming pot of something. Penelope suspected she intended the act to hide her nervousness at speaking against the king. After the queen died, Matilda and some of the other women of the castle had taken over more motherly roles.

"I know he does." Penelope spied a basket on the counter and peeked inside to find all sorts of delectables. "Is this for me?"

"Oh yes, dear. The boys packed their own supplies for you, but I put together some of your favorites. Hopefully, they'll keep your body nourished, as well as your heart."

Penelope slipped her arm into the handle of the basket, balanced it in the crook of her arm, and then kissed the cook on her cheek. "Thank you, for everything. And when I return, hopefully we'll have even more to celebrate."

Matilda's eyes crinkled at the corners, and sparkled anew. "Ah, yes, that would be a fine day. Cooking for thy wedding."

Penelope laughed. "I haven't even left and come back yet, and you have me married off. You are as bad as father."

With a wink of her eye, she left the kitchen, and placed the supplies in the hall. She had one last duty before she embarked—saying good-bye to all of her siblings. At least it was early enough they would still be sleeping. Fewer dramatics.

Softly, she stepped into each room and placed a kiss on their foreheads. When she reached Gwennie's room, her chest tightened. So young and innocent. She needed someone to watch over her more than anyone. Was she being selfish in leaving?

I need this one thing before I settle down. One adventure, and then I can return to focusing on them.

She needed to keep telling herself that, or else she'd never leave. After her bath the night before, Gwennie had smelled like fresh flowers and a spring day. As she kissed her forehead, Penelope inhaled the scent, memorizing it. The little miss opened her eyes.

"Good morn." She rubbed away the sleep.

"Shhhh. It's all right." Penelope brushed back her hair, cooing to her. "Go back to sleep. Love you."

As she turned over, Gwen murmured, "Love you." Penelope's heart filled with love.

Outside, the men accompanying her on the journey had readied the horses. The king stood near Midnight, waiting for her.

"Father." She nodded, and braced for whatever he might say.

"You know I'm not fond of you leaving on a wild goose chase," he said.

"I know, but from the looks of it, you're sending half the kingdom with me. It'll be like I never left."

The corners of his mouth tugged upward, as if he fought a smile. "I can't have my girl taking off on her own. It wouldn't be safe or proper."

At that comment, he looked over her attire. She'd dressed in loose breeches and an oversized men's shirt. Her hair was pulled back and she meant to tuck it under a hat. "I see you're venturing in disguise, too?"

She patted her hair. "It seems safer, for now. I don't know what to expect."

He gave the briefest nod of his head, and held out a purple velvet pouch. "Coin for your journey. Don't want for any comfort, and if you need anything, send word."

He leaned in for a kiss, and soft whiskers

brushed her cheek. "Come home soon, my girl, and I hope you find whatever it is you're searching for."

***

The first part of the day passed uneventfully. With two men riding in front of her and three behind, Penelope didn't really feel like she was on her own. As the sun drew close to setting, they approached a small village. The head guard raised his hand, and brought his horse beside hers.

"Milady, 'tis a good time to stop. Before nightfall, and with a warm place to stay." He gestured toward an inn a few doors down. "Is it to your liking?"

She wanted to press on, and keep riding until they were ready to fall off the horses. She'd rather sleep on soft grass, underneath a tree and the wide open skies, but as she looked around at the other men's faces, she knew she'd be the only one who felt that way. They were indulging her on this excursion. They saw no need for added hardships. While a mutiny was unlikely, she decided she'd better go with the flow. Later, if necessary, she'd force the issue.

"Sounds good," she said. "Why don't you go reserve the rooms and see what's for dinner? We'll follow."

He nodded, and took off at a trot. The village—if it could be called that—featured a smattering of buildings lining the road, with some houses set out behind. Paint flaked off the grocery merchant's store, and loud rumblings escaped from the salon. A man with a tankard of ale watched them warily as they passed. Maybe it wouldn't be such a good idea to stop here after all. Weary from the all-day ride, Penelope decided not to push it, but she was thankful to be wearing a disguise.

She swung her leg over Midnight, and dismounted. Two groomsmen immediately slid off their horses in order to help. She shooed them away, and pulled the legs of her pants out of her crotch. She hadn't foreseen walking like she had a stick up her....

FORTUNES READ. The sign hung in the inn window, enticing passersby. What might she learn about her the journey?

The head guardsman, Erik, opened the door, and gestured for Penelope to enter. As she stepped through the entranceway, a spell of dizziness overtook her. She swayed and grasped the nearest chair for support.

"Whoa, my lady. Are you all right?" One hand on her elbow and the other on the side of her waist, Erik caught her.

Feeling more steady, she nodded. "Thank you. Not sure what happened there. Must have been the long ride."

"Could be. It's good we stopped for the night."

"Perhaps, after all."

The interior was dark, the bare windows covered in a thick coat of grime that kept out the setting sun. The downstairs part of the establishment served food, and a handful of the tables were taken. Pea assumed the staircase along the back must lead up to the bedrooms. Penelope turned toward the right, drawn toward the call of the fortuneteller.

"Miss?" Erik called. "I've checked you into a room. If you'd like to go upstairs to freshen up...."

She held up a hand. "If you give me a few moments, I'll follow. I'd like to make a stop first."

"It's not good to mess with fate," he warned. He must have seen the direction she took.

"I'm not planning on messing with fate, just seeing what the wicked mistress of the future has in store for me," she replied. "Now if you'll excuse me."

Red chiffon shrouded the fortuneteller's alcove. The material hanging over the windows of this room added to the allure, and the light coming in cast a warm glow. Lit candles dotted the rich wood shelving, adding to the ambiance.

Penelope ventured farther inside, running her hand along the round table and feeling the contours worn by time.

"Hello. Is there anyone here?" she called out. Her voice echoed in the room, and a chill ran up her spine. *Someone walking over my grave.* Maybe Erik's recommendation to bypass this excursion was a good one.

Just as she was about to leave, a man emerged from a curtained-off area. "Hello, fine sir. How can I help you?"

She suppressed a giggle, remembering how she was dressed. "I'm looking for the woman who reads fortunes."

"Ah, I see. What a high voice you have for a gentleman. And you assume only women can see the future?"

"Well, no. I guess I never thought of it before. I'm sorry."

He gestured toward the chair on the opposite side of the table. "Come, sit and tell me what bothers you."

She looked closer at him. His light-brown hair brushed his shoulders, and was curled up at the ends.

While tall, his form was slender, and his clothes appeared well worn but clean. The ruffled neck of his forest-green shirt flared open, exposing a hairy chest. His dark brown pants snugged tight against narrow hips. She listened to her other senses. She was safe within the hotel, with her father's men within calling distance. She didn't fear the man, and from his appearance, he seemed harmless enough. She took the offered seat.

In the close setting, he peered at her face and reached over the table. "If you don't mind...." He reached across the table and removed her hat. "Someone seems to be hiding her true identity, which may make this endeavor a bit harder."

"My apologies, sir. Not hiding per se. Merely traveling, and we'd only just arrived."

He took the explanation easily enough. "I see. May I have your hand? So you are on a great journey," he began.

Great insight. She had said they were traveling. She held her tongue, waiting for him to continue.

"Your dreaming is plagued by nightmares. There is something you fear greatly."

She leaned forward. "Can you see what it is? I can never see it clearly."

He shook his head. "It's not something in your past. I see it as something in your future."

Great. Future unknown. "I'm tired all the time. But I keep pushing through. I'm afraid to sleep."

"But to dream, you must sleep. And to reach your destiny, you must dream." He tilted her hand toward the light.

She thought of the woman she'd met in the other-world the night before. Penelope had the feeling she knew the woman. Briar Rose? That would be impossible. Right?

"What of my journey? Will I be successful?" She didn't want to tell him her plans outright, but some indication her adventure would be worthwhile might be nice.

"The end result is based upon many elements and is ever-changing." He ran the tip of his finger along her palm, tracing a line. "I see some obstacles. Whatever happens, you need to have faith it's the right outcome. You just need to trust me."

"On this?" The muscles of her stomach clenched. She should follow her instincts. "I make my own future."

The fortuneteller dropped her hand and sat back in his chair, observing her. The weight of his gaze followed her, and Penelope held still. What did he see?

"Are you out to rescue another, or yourself?"

The truth of his question hit close to home. Sure, she had a specific destination in mind—the Holy Grail of freeing the cursed princess. But, on the journey, she also hoped to discover her path in life.

"I thank you for your time." She fumbled with the drawstring purse. She placed a coin on the table, not bothering to ask for the cost of the reading, and stood to leave.

Without looking down, he closed his hand over the payment. "Wait a moment. I have one thing to aid you along the way."

From behind him, he opened a drawer and removed a small pouch of brilliant red. He pushed it across the table toward her. "In here are some magic pills. Some tiny purveyors of energy. If you feel the journey is drawing too much of your energy, take one—or two—and you will be able to go on without sleep. But know there is a price to pay. Neither the body nor the mind can go too long without rest."

The pouch felt warm in her hand, and she tucked it into her purse. An image of Sleeping Beauty lying in wait came to her mind. "But sometimes too much sleep isn't a good thing either."

"Then seek balance. Now, go get some rest. The next few days will try you in a variety of ways."

Penelope stumbled out of the alcove, only to find Erik waiting outside. "From the look on your face, you don't like what you heard," he said. "Come on, let's get you settled."

She didn't have the strength to fight him again, and let him lead her upstairs. She sat upon the lumpy bed, and patted the covers. At least no dust greeted her movements.

"You rest. I'll have dinner sent up, and don't think about getting a wild hair and taking off anywhere. We'll be in the rooms next to you," he directed.

Settling back against the pillows, she shut her eyes and thought about the tangled words of the fortuneteller and what remained to be done.

***

Despite the sun shining above, Briar Rose felt no radiating warmth. The experiences within her dream world possessed a bitter edge. So much better than the darkness, that dreary emptiness filling her life. She craved to live life in vibrant detail with all her senses afire. Oh, how she missed those elements.

She drifted in limbo from one scene to the next, sometimes directed to a memory, a repeated charm of happiness, like her mom surprising her with a mini rose-decorated cake on her birthday morning. Other times, though, the experience turned toward the unknown, like the woman, Penelope, she encountered in the glen. Was the princess really on a quest to rescue her? What were the odds a princess would succeed?

The setting before her shifted, as if thinking about the woman brought her to this interlude.

"So we meet again." Penelope drew closer.

Side by side, they lay on a soft blanket pillowed by sweet grasses. The smell of spring filled the air, and Rose clung to the sensory elements. Somehow, someway, this woman made life richer, as if she truly were alive again. If she reached out, she'd be able to touch her. Feel.

"Where are you now?" Briar asked, searching the would-be rescuer's face. "How do you find me here?"

"I close my eyes, and there you are," Penelope explained. Slowly, she trailed her fingertips up Briar's bare arm, until it intersected with the curve of her breast. "Where I am now? On the way to meet you in person. I keep my promises. Right now, can't we think of a better way to spend our time?"

The combination of touch and Penelope's words quickened Briar's pulse. She shivered, not from the cold but from anticipation.

In a blink, the scene and their positions changed. Penelope took control of the dream, and found herself between the sleeping beauty's legs. Penelope spread the petals and watched the dew of the lush nether lips glisten, as pink as any delicate rose. She dipped her head for a taste. She flicked the tip of her tongue over Rose's clit, and the other woman squirmed beneath her attention.

"Like that, do you? There will be much more where that came from," she said.

"I do not know..." Briar protested, lifting her head and attempting to close her plush pale thighs. All around her, the long skirt of her dress billowed like a full-body halo.

Even more insistent, Penelope braced her elbows on Briar's knees, keeping them propped open. "Yes, you can take it, and as much as I can give you. And then more."

Swirl, lick, and suck. Pea fell into a pattern, set at bringing Rose to climax as quickly as possible. She mirrored her movements to Rose's breathing patterns. She wasn't the most vocal lover, but Pea took her cues from the woman's body language.

"Ready for more?" Penelope asked.

Wide blue eyes greeted her question. Her pale-blonde hair fanned out on the golden parts of the blanket behind her head, blending into the scenery.

"I don't think so."

"And that means yes."

Slowly, she slid one slick finger into Rose's tight channel, relishing the sucking sensation as the pale beauty's inner walls held onto her appendage. With her thumb, she caressed the magic button, hoping to increase the sensations. When the movement grew smooth, she added in a second finger, and finally a third, until she finger-banged full force.

"Oh, fuck me." Briar tossed her head side to side with every other thrust of Pea's fingers.

"That's kind of the idea," she returned.

Sliding up Rose's body, Penelope kissed the other woman's mouth, their tongues tangling until both of them broke to suck in some much-needed air.

Briar's thigh muscles tensed beneath Penelope's hand. She was going to come, and fast.

The key was to let go and enjoy the moment. Penelope was doing her best to learn that lesson. As the other woman lay beneath her, her face flushed with pleasure and mouth open in climax, Penelope filled with satisfaction. She'd done that—brought pleasure to another.

And as quickly, the elements around her faded. Penelope woke to a whispered, "Thank you," in her mind and knocking on the room's door.

"Time to wake, miss," the guardsman called out. "We must be on our journey."

As she dressed, Penelope planned out the best way to ditch her escorts.

Chapter Four

L ater that evening, after the entire team settled down for another night, Penelope popped a few of her energy pills and snuck off on Midnight. Heart racing from the escape, she rode the horse for a few hours, until guilt for her steed's care overrode her drive. She followed the sound of a murmuring stream and unpacked for a few hours' rest.

Above, the sky sparkled with bright stars. Arms folded behind her head, Penelope gazed at the heavens, and wondered what the world around Briar Rose was like. That night, sleep did not come. She skirted around the edges of the dream-world, hoping for another encounter with the sweet princess Rose. Alas, she'd ingested one—or two—pills too many for her mind to stop wandering and her body to settle down. The hours stretched by, one by one, until exhaustion set in.

Dawn came not in a slow show of bright pink, yellow, and orange splendor but in an onslaught of brilliance. Yawning, Penelope fed Midnight a serving of oats and checked his hooves for any stray pebbles.

By the stream, she splashed water on her face then dried it off with the back of her sleeve. She finger-combed her hair and tied it back with a string of leather. The weight of the adventure pressed against her eyelids, and she struggled to stay awake.

Today would be the day. She felt it, deep in her soul. Somehow, she knew she had to make this last part of the journey alone, without the accompaniment of the men. In order to make it there, though, she would have to take a few more of those energy pills. Otherwise, she'd fall asleep right on the horse.

Before long, she pressed on, an increased sense of urgency fueling her determination. Temptations of songbirds and landscapes to entice a pleasant rest held no power. Penelope rode until Midnight stopped before an overgrown hedge, thick with thorns. Dismounting, she gazed upward. If necessary, she'd scale it, but she'd rather not cause undue harm to her hands.

Watching each step, she walked the wall, looking for a break in the foliage. *Where else would one keep a princess but inside a castle behind an overgrown forest?*

Meooooow.

A cat? Ahead, a black and white cat sat on the grass licking its paw. *What is a cat doing out here?* He stood, stretched out his back in an arch, and flicked the end of his tail. He turned and lazily walked in the opposite direction. After a few feet, he stopped to look at Penelope, as if to say, *Are you going to follow me?*

"I'm coming," she muttered. "Why the hell not. I've come this far. Might as well take directions from a feline."

Rawer, the cat replied, before taking off again.

Ten minutes later, when she was ready to give up on the futility of looking for an easy way in, the four-legged guide slipped through the vines and disappeared. Penelope trotted to the spot and lifted her arms.

"Great. Thanks for your help! You know, you're much smaller than me, right?"

No way my ass will fit through the narrow space, but it's better than going over. She surveyed the possibilities.

First, she removed her outer shirt and used it to cover her head and sides of her face. Turning sideways, she did her best to condense her body and stepped in.

Sharp thick branches cut into her from all sides. No worry. Since it resembled overgrown climbing roses, the plant embracing the castle's walls shouldn't be deadly, nor would the pain be permanent. She gritted her teeth. Her pants snagged on a persistent bramble, and an overwhelming sense of being trapped blanketed her senses. The covering on her face tightened, blocking her view. Instinctively, she reached up to move it aside and found she couldn't move her arm.

Stuck. Her breathing became shallow, and she gulped for air. She wasn't getting out. *Father's men will find me here, dead and withered.*

Get a grip. She'd never been prone to hysterics. Inches at a time, she moved her fingers and hand backward until she squeezed the material of her pants. Holding her breath, she counted one-two-three in her head and jerked her body to the side.

Riiiiip. Freedom. *There go my pants.* She flailed at her hair, ridding herself of the claustrophobic shroud. Pain radiated down her arms in a few spots, and she blotted the trails of blood before putting her shirt back on and tying it at the waist. She checked the damage to her pants. They'd hold up. She patted the bag of magic beans. It was measurably lighter than when she'd left.

Before her stood a once-magnificent castle. Not too large, and not too small. *Just right.* A wide moat circled the structure, and a narrow bridge connected here to there. Tendrils of ivy grew from thick trunks, overgrown to the size of a strong man's thigh, climbing the walls of the castle. Toward the very top, light streamed from a window with open shutters. Penelope surveyed the structure.

What do you want to bet that's where the princess is kept? She weighed her options. Certainly, there were enchantments or guards overseeing the grounds? Warily, she approached the bridge, expecting it to disappear and dump her in the water. Nothing. She reached the front door. *Shall I knock and call out if anyone's home?* She turned the tarnished handle and found the door easily swung open. Why would they need to lock up?

For being essentially abandoned, the marble floors shimmered under the light following her indoors. To the right, a staircase wound up in a semi-circle. As she stood in the foyer, another decision loomed. Either she went upstairs or checked the downstairs rooms first. With a glimpse toward the hallway on her right toward a sitting area, she disregarded the option. She had to be in the topmost room. That's what made the most sense. *No need to waste time now.*

You're the "weaker sex." What hope do you have to accomplish something now? What makes you think a princess will be lying in wait for you up there? Even more so, who says she's ever going to want you?

Doubts plagued Penelope with each step up the stairs. At the landing, she stopped to catch her breath and take in the surroundings. Gold and white-striped paper peeled off the walls. She lost count of steps on the way up and finally reached the second floor. A thick layer of dust clung to every shelf in the hallway. Bizarre compared to the first. Nose itching and eyelids heavy, she pressed on, up the narrow stairwell to the tower. Only the front half of her foot fit on the steps. By the time she reached the top, the width of her shoulders almost touched the walls on either side.

Finally, the moment arrived. The door to her future lay before her. Once Penelope walked through it, all would change. She'd never go back to being the person she was before. Fail or succeed, it didn't matter. Soon, reality would come crashing back. For now, she remained a hero.

In the room, nature battled humanity for occupancy. An abundance of vines and greenery crawled in through the window, covered the walls, and climbed up and around the raised bed. The area looked like someone had transported the bed into the middle of the forest. Penelope's heart lifted. She'd accomplished the hard task—finding Briar Rose. Now for the next step—waking her. The floor creaked as Penelope approached the sleeping figure.

Foot lifted, she paused, waiting to see if something might happen. The hairs on her arm stood at attention, and she got the uneasy feeling someone watched her every movement. *Where did that damn cat go anyway?*

White roses curled over the pedestals of the four-poster bed. Tendrils of green laced over the woman's feet and legs. Soon enough, she'd be encased and returned to nature. It couldn't be too late—not yet.

The princess's pink lips looked so soft and delicate. Her golden curls sparkled in the sunlight streaming in through the window. Penelope reached out, tempted to touch, and wound her finger through one curl.

Skeeeth! A ginormous black and white cat hissed, leaping at Penelope's outstretched hand, and slashed its nails across the back of her freckled skin.

"Oww," she yelled, pulling back. "You evil beast!"

Too late. The damage had already been done. Drops of blood dripped over the roses, and Penelope blinked her eyes.

What the...?

The blood appeared to be spreading. The red of her blood transformed the roses into a pale pink—the color of Briar Rose's lips.

The offending feline leapt straight at Penelope, and she shrieked, dodging to the side. The cat crash-landed behind her and dashed off to parts unknown.

Good riddance.

The sound of a sharp intake of breath drew her attention to the sleeping maiden. Wide blue eyes lay open, searching around until they landed on Penelope's face. She hadn't kissed her, and yet Briar Rose was awake.

"You." Rose's voice rasped after years of disuse.

"Yes, me," she said, returning to the bedside. She

trailed her fingertips down the side of Rose's face.

"I dreamt of you." A soft blush spread up her chest and across her cheeks. "So many times."

"I thought I was the only one." Those dreams had inspired Penelope to make this trek and risk everything if only to find and free the princess. When she started out, she had no idea what she'd find at the end of her journey, but, as the dreams continued...oh, she'd hoped.

The woman of her fantasies strained against the vines binding her, and coughed. "My throat. So dry."

Idiot! Penelope fumbled with the water bottle strapped to her side and brought it to Rose's lips. Just because they looked plump and delectable didn't mean she wasn't thirsty. She drank.

"Slow. It's been a long time."

"Thank you." She attempted to raise her arms but couldn't do much more than move them. "Can you help me with these?"

"Sure thing." She brought out her pocketknife. "Hold still. I wouldn't want to hurt you."

A weak laugh escaped her dream lover's mouth. "I don't imagine that being a problem at the moment."

Penelope set to work on the tendrils on one arm. Despite not doing Rose any harm, the thorns plucked at her fingers, as if purposely trying to hurt her.

"Ow!" She stuck her index finger into her mouth, and sucked off the blood. The roses turned a darker shade. Now, they were more magenta. *Keep this up and they'll be blood-red by the time we get out of here.*

Remembering her promise to Gwennie, she tucked one of the roses into her satchel. Perhaps it possessed some sort of magical quality. If anything, the crimson-stained petals were one of a kind and a symbol of this adventure.

"What's going on? Did you see that?" Rose asked. When her one free hand, she picked up a few loose petals that had fallen on her chest. "These are white, and yet the others turned a dark pink. Didn't they?"

"I can't explain it," Penelope said, "but they seem to like my blood. Along with that evil cat of yours."

"Puss? Is Puss here?" She whistled as if calling a reasonable pet like a dog or a horse. Who expected a cat to come on command? "Here, kitty-kitty."

No answer.

"It was. After the blasted thing scratched me, it took off."

"He. Puss is a he, and he's got to be around here somewhere. He's never left my side."

"Good riddance," Penelope mumbled under her breath, and then set to work on the vines along Rose's ankles. She slipped the blade under each branch and cut upward. Soon enough, she was free.

Carefully, one hand supporting Rose's lower back and the other holding onto her hand, Penelope helped her down from the bed. She swayed on weak legs.

"Oh my. It feels like it's been years since I last stood." The princess wobbled as she found her balance.

"It has. You don't want to know how long."

She stilled. "Do I dare ask?"

"Later. Right now, let's get out of here. I've got a bad feeling."

The branches she'd cut trembled, shriveling and constricting. Like a wave, Penelope watched the movement start at those closest to them and flow outward toward the window. She mentally flashed toward an image of all the greenery covering the outside walls of the caste. Were they all connected?

Bam! The room shook with a violent vibration. Rose swayed, falling into Penelope's waiting arms. She caught her. For a moment, they stared into each other's eyes. Penelope focused on her lips. Those soft, beautiful lips. The other woman lifted up on her tip toes until they were but a breath apart.

They kissed. Magic exploded behind Penelope's closed eyelids. Sparkles and glitter and this feeling of rightness coiled within her belly and zigzagged through her entire system. This. Her. She tasted like sweetened roses, and the scent of her filled her nose and mouth. Penelope slipped one hand around Rose's slender waist, enjoying the softness of her velvet gown. The princess gave a soft moan against her mouth, and the earth moved.

Wait. The earth moved, and not only from the kiss. The shaking broke them apart, and Rose stepped back, fingertips to her lips.

"We'll have more of that later," Penelope said. "Right now, though, we have to get out of here before the whole place crumbles around us."

"I can't leave Puss!" she insisted. "Here kitty-kitty."

"It's a cat. He'll survive, get out on his own." Penelope hadn't come this far to get hung up on a pet. She grabbed Rose's hand and led her out of the room.

The princess cast a longing glance around her room—or prison—and followed. "Puss, come on, boy. We need to go."

Silence.

A tall cabinet filled with precious porcelain toppled behind them with a crash. Penelope turned, taking in the shattered figurines.

"Oh." Rose knelt to grab one that was still intact. She cupped her hand around the statue of a ballerina. "I loved this one as a child," she explained, before slipping it inside her pocket.

"You can love it more if we make it out alive." Penelope encouraged her to move faster.

A thunderous clatter shook the walls of the castle. Sediment rained from the ceiling, covering Rose and Penelope in gritty silt.

"Ack!" Rose exclaimed, shaking her long blonde curls. She steadied a hand against the staircase railing.

Meoooow. A screech came from the level above, and Rose glanced up and about-faced.

After seeing the determination in her dream lover's wide blue eyes, Penelope reached out to grab her. She touched the pink velvet trim of her darker pink cape and then nothing as it slipped through her fingers.

"Curse it!" Penelope stomped her foot. "We have to get to safety," she called up the stairs. Her voice chased the retreating form of the princess.

After all we've been through, we're going to die—all because of that blasted cat. Rooawwww.

No way she was letting Rose go back up alone. Not with the entire history of the fairy tale crashing around them. Penelope gathered her courage, and charged the stairs.

But something happened about a third of the way up. She staggered, the tip of a toe catching on the lip of one stair, and she went down, her knees slamming against the hard floor. "Ugh!"

The desire for sleep, to slip into oblivion, overtook Penelope. *No! Not now.* She clutched at her purse, digging for her energy pills...and came out with nothing. Impossible. She couldn't be out. She upended the satchel, spilling its contents onto the step. She checked the seams. Empty.

Doomed. The villagers would find their bodies buried in the castle and laugh at the audacity of two women trying to escape the curse of a decade.

Pea heard a loud, blood-curdling scream. *Briar Rose.* Fear spread through the pit of Penelope's belly. She fought the wave of tiredness.

No way. She opened the purse and shoved all the items inside. She gathered her resolve to push on, and attempted to stand. Another jolt rocked the castle, and she grabbed the banister to keep from tumbling backward.

Dammit. She was getting up there, even if she had to crawl up the stairs—exactly what she was going to do.

Two-thirds of the way up a splintering sound from behind stopped her ascent. *That sounds bad.* Although afraid, she looked back. A chasm separated the staircase—not too big it would be impossible to jump over...it didn't widen even more.

By the time she reached the landing, Rose stood there, a purring cat in her arms. She stroked its hair, cooing, and Penelope swore the cat looked at her with pure satisfaction in its eyes. If the cat could speak, he'd be saying, "Na, na, na, na."

She pushed down the jealousy and focused. "The cat. I can't believe you risked your life, and mine, for that cat, and we're still not out of here."

"He's more than a cat," Rose explained. "He's my brother."

"What?" Pure shock and surprise. She glanced at the animal. "You mean 'I love him so much he's like a brother'?"

"No. My actual brother. He broke the wrong woman's heart. The same witch who cursed me to sleep transformed him into a cat. I couldn't leave him behind."

"Beg pardon, Sir Puss." Penelope sounded as silly as she felt. "Now can we get out of here?"

A crash sounded from below. The crack had widened and splintered. "Well, there goes our way out." The remaining energy drained out of Penelope. "Now what?"

Rooooaaar, the cat sounded.

"Oh, good idea," Rose said. "The servants' entrance. Quick, follow me—this way."

"You understand the cat? No, wait. Forget about it."

Chapter Five

The walls shook with a thunderous clatter. Pea planted her hand against the stone, hoping against hope the castle would hold until they made their exit.

"Who dares shatter my curse?" the voice of a woman called out. "How dare you defy me?"

Briar Rose squeezed Penelope's hand and pressed a finger to her lips. "Shhh," she whispered. "Don't let her know where we are. Otherwise, we'll never escape."

The damned cat stroked in and out between Briar's ankles, in a bit of a tizzy. She reached down and petted its back, giving reassuring murmurs. Penelope refrained from giving it a good square...well, its purring was so loud the woman behind the giant voice would hear it.

"Come," Briar urged. "We must keep going. I know a secret passage under the moat."

Convenient. Of course there would be a way to go under it rather than over. When they reached the bottom of the stairs, with light shining through the doorway and salvation right there in the sun's rays,

Briar tugged her toward the left. She let Briar lead the way.

As they turned the corner past the grand ballroom, a wall of rubble greeted their way. Dust polluted the air, and Penelope attempted to sweep it away with her free hand. Briar sank to the floor, her skirts pooling perfectly about her body.

"I don't know what I'm thinking. I'm only a girl, not a superhero. I don't have any special powers to get us out of here," she said.

The strength of determination set in, overwriting exhaustion. No way in hell had Penelope come this far only to be deterred by some spilled rocks.

"I don't think so." She tugged at Briar. "Haven't you spent enough time trapped in this prison? Get up. I don't have the strength to carry you out of here, but why should I when you have two perfectly working legs."

With determination, Penelope jiggled the nearest rock that looked like it could move without taking everything else down around them. She shifted it and pushed it aside then attacked the next one. After a few successes, she turned toward Briar.

"Come on, help me. We're not going anywhere with only me doing the work."

Brushing off her hands on her skirts, Briar stood and came alongside her. "Puss, can you jump up in that crack and scout? Is the rest of the way clear?"

Meow. The feline did exactly as directed. He disappeared into the shadows only to reemerge a few moments later with a flick of his tail.

"Do you think you're going to be able to escape me?" the woman's voice roared. "If you don't come out to me, then I'll have to come get you."

Debris clattered from the ceiling, sending Briar into a coughing fit. When the residue settled, a fine covering of gray ghosted them both. Penelope tore a strip of material from the bottom of her shirt and tied the rest into a knot. Great, now she resembled one of those young women trying to be too sexy too soon. Who cared?

With the softest touch, she wiped Briar's face with one end of the strip of fabric. "Here, take a sip of my water." She offered her flask. "Clear your throat."

The proper princess took the smallest sip, frustrating Penelope further. "Like this," she said, demonstrating. The lukewarm wake streamed over her lips and down the sides of her throat. Fine, right now, it was a bit wasteful, but the other woman needed to learn to let go. It wasn't always about being delicate.

Why do I care? An inner voice of reason peppered her with questions. If she were a knight doing the rescuing, she'd have tossed Briar over her shoulder and set off long ago. A knight wouldn't worry about an evil sorceress lurking outside threatening them. He'd draw his sword, do away with the evil woman, and disappear into the sunset with his prize.

Alas, she didn't have those qualifications. But, then again, she'd gotten further than any man had, and she had done so by not following the preconceived rules.

"Are you ready to keep going?" she prodded.

Briar nodded. Penelope ripped another piece of the shirt and tied it as a makeshift mask over Briar's face. "To help filter out the dust," she explained.

The other woman's blue eyes sparkled with

moisture, and she nodded.

Together, they moved the stones aside one by one, forging an escape route. Soon, they'd cleared enough to slide through. The question would be whether to send Briar first, or go herself to make sure the other side was safe. The voice of the sorceress kept coming from somewhere behind them. It seemed safer to go forward.

"Are you ready?" Penelope asked.

Without further instructions, the cat—now more gray than black and white—jumped to the top of the wall and disappeared. A soft thud reverberated from the other side, and he meowed.

"My turn." Briar ran the palm of her hand across Penelope's cheek. "No matter what happens, I can't thank you enough for saving me. I never expected to be rescued, and you were—you are—more than I could have dreamed of."

She leaned forward and pressed the softest of kisses against Penelope's mouth. A sizzle of sensation shot through her body. *Magic.*

This feeling of satisfaction, of anticipation, was what everyone had always been talking about. It was what the king wanted her to discover while dancing with a prince from a neighboring kingdom during the ball. Something had directed Pea on this journey. More than the desire to escape her everyday life. She'd risked so much, and the prize.... Well, the prize might prove extra plentiful.

"Thank you," Pea said. "For having faith in me. Now, before it's too late, you slip through there and I'll be close behind."

With a final nod, Briar placed her hands on the rocks and began to climb. Once she reached the top, she looked down. Penelope smiled and then Briar disappeared in a cacophony of falling stones.

"Briar!" she called out, scrambling to the top. Her nail caught on a rock, and ripped off, shooting pain down her index finger. She sucked on the tip briefly then finished the climb. "Briar, answer me."

A soft coughing sound came in reply and a feline *Meeeeooooow*.

Darkness greeted Penelope on the other side. She waited a few moments for her vision to adjust then eyed Briar's form on the floor. The helpless woman act grew a bit old. She knelt beside her and pressed her fingertips against the pulse in her neck. Nice and steady.

In the darkness, the damn cat hissed and stalked forward.

"Oh, hush, you. By now you have to know I don't mean her any harm. Plus, you led me to her. I'm checking to make sure she's alive…she's okay."

The cat circled Briar, flicking its tail against her arm and her face. Soon enough, she brushed the fur aside and sat up.

"Again? Oh I'm sorry. Being locked up in this place has done a job on me," she explained. "It must be residual effects from the spell. I feel weak."

The muscles along Penelope's shoulders loosened as Briar's words sank in. "Well that, and you haven't used your body in a long time," she offered.

"Too long," Briar joked. "Still, I'm frustrated by the limitations of my body." She lifted one hand in the air. "Here, help me up, and let's get the hell out of here."

Once they reached the secret exit, Briar removed a key from a chain around her neck. Someone had carved intricate flowers into the wooden door. Penelope moved closer, running her fingers along the detail. *Roses, of course.*

"You really meant secret, didn't you?" Penelope asked.

"Consider this the official escape route, but Mama and Papa probably never imagined it being used in exactly such a strange way." Briar opened the lock, and the unused door creaked open.

"How could they otherwise?" Pea asked.

"We used it more for bringing supplies in to the castle. You know, so as to not mess everything else up," she explained.

They talked as they walked, and soon filtered light shone in the distance. The confirmation of nearing the end made them pick up the pace. Puss dashed out before them, with Briar fast on his tail.

"Wait," Penelope warned, grabbing at Briar's arm. The silky fabric slipped through her fingers. Fear nagged at Pea's consciousness. If it wasn't actually a "secret passage," but used for household duties, then others probably knew....

A scream pierced her reflection.

"Briar." She stepped into full sunshine, shielding her eyes against the sudden brightness.

"Well, well, well. Look what we have here." A creature best described as a misshapen woman held Briar with an arm around her chest, feet off the ground. "My little princess somehow escaped." Her laugh echoed, killing all the sounds of the forest.

"Let me go! You have no right!" Briar kicked her feet and fought against the strong arm holding her.

"Oh, I think I do. Where's that mangy brother of yours? He should never have dumped me! Is he tired of being a cat yet? Maybe I should turn him into a frog."

"You leave him alone." Briar kicked out, her legs failing to make contact and lashing in the wind.

She's the witch who transformed Puss? What taste in women he had. Maybe he deserved what happened to him. No wonder he hid somewhere at the moment. Penelope searched him out, inside nearby bushes, for an ally in this attack.

"Now I wonder, how did you break my curse? No prince should have been able...." In slow motion, she turned to gaze at Penelope and cold seeped over her body and into her soul.

Black despair like she hadn't experienced since the death of her mom assaulted her emotions, and deep exhaustion set in. She reached into her bag out of habit, searching for another magic berry. She came up empty.

Behind her lay the dark tunnel. A rumbling sounded from the sky, and bricks from a turret crashed down. The wicked witch stood between Pea and her future. Where had Puss run off to? Probably hiding in one of the bushes. He'd be of no help. She didn't even have to look back to weigh her options. There was no other path.

"You?" The sorceress dropped Briar and advanced upon Penelope. She tilted her head to the side. "Interesting. A woman solved the mystery and broke my spell. A loophole. What magic powers do you have?"

"None," Penelope said. *If I had magic powers, how much of my life would I change?* "But I do have something you don't."

"And what is that?"

Some people, like Briar Rose, emanated a golden glow of goodness or happiness. The sorceress emitted a polluted shadow, like her unhappiness infected all around. How sad to live like that.

"I have hope." Power and energy surged within her. A burst of invincibility. She held up her arms, palms facing the woman, and shoved.

A beam of white light burst forth, shattering the blackness surrounding the sorceress. She screamed, pushing it away.

"What are you doing? It burns."

"Hurry, Briar. Get behind me."

Briar moved to stand next to her.

"Help me," Penelope instructed.

"I don't understand." Briar watched her. "What are you doing? How are you doing that?"

"I'm not quite sure but think of all the love and kindness and hope in your heart. Let it fill you, and project that energy out," she said. As though enlivened by Pea's words, her light shone brighter.

Beside her, Briar closed her eyes and lifted her face to the sun. How wonderful the warmth must feel after being secluded for so many years inside. Her arm pressed against Penelope's and, when she opened her eyes, they sparkled anew. She held out her hands and a shimmer of glittery pink burst forth, accompanied by a crackling sound, and joined Penelope's beam. Really? Even Briar's energy was filled with glamour.

A glowing bubble enveloped the sorceress, trapping her within positive energy until the bubble exploded. She stumbled, holding her hand up to the side of her head, and Penelope didn't wait to see the end result.

She grabbed Briar's hand. "We better run, and call that cat of yours."

"Here, kitty-kitty-kitt—" Her call cut off as Penelope tugged.

Penelope looked back and noticed something odd. The black cloud surrounding the sorceress had disappeared. Her aura shone with a violet glow. *What does that mean?*

"Me-ow." Puss leaped out of a bush and joined their retreat. As they reached the outside of the moat, Penelope untied her horse from his post, mounted, and helped Briar climb on. The princess stroked and soothed Midnight, and the stallion tilted his ears back to listen. Of course she'd have a special knack, with even Penelope's horse, who'd never liked anybody but her.

As for the cat, he'd have to walk alongside them. She couldn't imagine carrying him back for the journey. Besides, the horse wouldn't think of it.

They set off at a brisk pace. Headed home, with the prized possession of the princess, Penelope saw no reason to meander. The faster, the better.

Briar wrapped her arms around Penelope's middle and pressed her luscious breasts against her back. It was sheer distraction, but thankfully Midnight seemed to know his way home. She didn't have to do much guiding.

"I never thought I'd ever be outside again," Briar said. "Thank you so very much for saving me, for saving us."

"Your pleasure is my pleasure," she said.

"Oooh, look at the beautiful meadow." Briar pointed at a nestled oval of soft grasses and wildflowers. "May we stop and pick some flowers?"

After Briar had been cooped up for so long, Pea understood why she wanted to explore a little bit. Maybe the way home wouldn't be quite so quick after all.

***

From Midnight's pack, Penelope removed a soft blanket from the finest sheep's wool and laid out on the grass. Briar and Penelope rested. Briar ran her hand over the colorful weave, remembering a dream similar to this encounter. After laying out a spread of slightly stale bread and aged meat from her saddlebags, the two of them ate. Puss struck out for a bit of hunting of his own, leaving them alone.

Her brother had spent so much of his time watching over and protecting her, he deserved a break. Free of the curse, one of her next priorities would be to break his.

When Penelope wasn't looking, Briar took in the strength of her jawline and the way she continuously checked their surroundings. For the first time in many years, she felt free and safe.

Each bite of food brought new pleasures—the crunch of the bread in her mouth and the feel of flaky crumbs falling onto her chest. She savored the sharp and salty spice of meat. Even the cool water refreshed from the stream running through the meadow invigorated her in a way Briar didn't remember. How could she have taken so much of life for granted before, even before the curse? She vowed not to let that happen again.

Stomach pleasantly full, she bunched up an edge of the blanket to use as a pillow. "Mmmm, thank you." Briar stretched, feeling the smile on her face. The world held unseen wonders, mysteries promising to unveil at the perfect moment. "I thought you were amazing in our dream world. In reality, you're much better."

Penelope propped up on her elbow. "How much do you remember of that?" She brushed the hair back from Briar's forehead and played with the silken strands.

A blush spread across her bosom and heated her cheeks. "All of it. Did you doubt it happened?" She reached to stroke the side of Penelope's face. The other woman's eyelashes fluttered shut, and she shivered. Briar focused on her mouth and completed the gesture with a soft kiss against her lips. "Once I saw you in our shared dreams, I knew we were destined to be together."

The admission questioned the foundation of reality and the other-world Penelope visited at night, the one that brought not only the pleasures of meeting with Briar Rose, but also the fears of the nightmares. *Wait. Could they have been about the evil sorceress?* She weighed the feeling against the all-too-real danger she'd recently encountered. Damn if the two didn't ring true.

Maybe all these years her dreams had been trying to tell her something and lead her upon the right path. She'd been running from them, and if she'd listened, maybe she would have found happiness sooner.

Afraid to sleep. If I'd only done the opposite?

"We were there, together. It was real." Pea gazed

off into the distance and grew quiet.

"A different type of real, I think. I can see you thinking," Briar said. "Stop it. Be happy for what we've found now, and don't fret so much about the past. Look at me, girl locked up in a castle for eternity...."

"You're right, now that I think about it. If that's the case, how can I take you from there to my kingdom? It'll be a different type of imprisonment. Maybe you should take some time in order to discover what you really want."

"Oh no you don't." Briar flipped her onto her back, pinning her hands slightly above her head. "Don't go running scared on me now. This conflict all of a sudden isn't on me. It's about you being afraid of what can happen between us. Are you ashamed for wanting me?"

"Wanting you? Not at all. Why would you say that?" Penelope struggled against the bonds holding her down. "My father, though...may not understand."

"You're not going anywhere." Briar shifted her weight to straddle Penelope's hips and unbuttoned her shirt. "I already have you figured out. You like to be in control, always. But guess what? Now it's my turn."

As a breeze flowed over Penelope's exposed skin, goose bumps broke out, only to be replaced with Briar's touch.

"With your name, I'd expect you to have some thorns but you're all soft without any rough edges," Pea teased.

"Ha, ha. As if I never heard that one before," she replied. "Do you remember what pricked you though?"

"Ah yes, now that you ask. Your brother's claws, and I bled the roses."

"Exactly. I think that was a bit of the magic that helped me finally escape. You didn't just kiss me, and expect to take something from me. You sacrificed your blood."

"Well, not by choice."

"Doesn't matter. It set you apart from everyone else, and, at that moment, I became part of you. We're now joined for all eternity, and even if you wanted to get rid of me, it would be pretty hard."

"Well, thankfully I don't see that happening any time in the future. What about other safeguards? Why do you think the sorceress didn't know I was there until too late?"

"Maybe she cast magic wards against potential rescuers who were men, but the spell was specific enough not to affect a woman." One by one, Briar slipped the straps of Penelope's chemise off her shoulders, exposing her pale breasts.

"Keep in mind...." Her voice faltered with the removal of clothes. "I may not be a traditional beauty like you—"

"Hush now, do you ever do anything besides talk?"

She attempted to escape once again, and Briar stopped her with a kiss. All cohesive thought left as they spun a new thread of their destiny web, overriding the role of the Fates. Briar ran her fingers up the inside seam of Penelope's pants, stopping to unhook the button.

"Lift your hips," she instructed, scooting them over her ass and discarding them to the side.

Truth be told, Briar Rose wasn't used to being nude with anybody—man or woman. Trust. In order to have any type of future, she needed to build trust, along with the desire, with this woman.

Rose smoothed her hands over Penelope's creamy thighs, as soft as the froth of freshly collected milk, memorizing each curve. She'd never touched another woman in such a manner, but she knew what felt good and—more than anything—wanted to grant pleasure.

Only after the proper homage did she dip her head and taste the offering. The tip of her tongue traversed a path from the knee upward. Right before she arrived at the juncture, she traveled and picked up on the other side.

"Tease," Pea complained, shifting her hips. She wound her fingers through Rose's hair, guiding her back to the cherished land.

"What's the matter?" Rose asked, laughing against the tense muscles of Pea's leg. "Am I missing something?"

"You know damn well. Rather than telling, why don't you show me how smart your mouth is?"

Oh I'll show you.

Rose slid her hand under Penelope's bare ass, lifting her slightly and holding her in place. If she wanted attention, she'd get it. With the other hand, she parted her rescuer's lips, exposing her engorged clit. Without further ado, she puckered her mouth and circled the nub, completely covering it, and sucked.

"That's it." Penelope bucked but, between her lover's hands and mouth, she didn't have far to move.

The scent of the lightest of spring flowers enveloped Rose as she licked and swirled her tongue.

"More, give me more."

Demanding minx, isn't she?

She stroked the soft folds of her opening, slipping in one, two, three fingers until the passage became tighter. Her appreciative grunts grew louder, encouraging Rose on.

"Like that, do you?"

"Yes, oh yes."

Raising up, she asked. "Did you ever doubt a princess could pleasure you as well as a prince?"

"Never." Her voice hitched, and a shudder vibrated through Penelope's body. "I always knew."

Dark clouds covered the sky, and the wind picked up. Briar Rose settled her clothes and patted her hair. Within moments, she'd erased all evidence of their liaison.

I'd like to see her truly come undone.

"Are you ready to go?" Penelope asked.

"Quite. After being alone for so long, it'll be good to get back to civilization."

"My men should be in a town a short distance from here." Pea could relate to the feeling. She'd been away from her family, and, no matter what awaited her return, it was time to face the future.

"Your men?" Briar asked. She placed her hand on her hip and cocked it. "I didn't realize you had *men.*"

"A kingdom doesn't run itself."

"Indeed." She turned toward the forest and cooed to her "kitty-kitty-kitty," and the damned thing crawled out from the brush.

Puss cleaned his paw, licking with an eye on

Penelope, as if he knew all too well what had been going on in the glen.

Grabbing hold of the horn, Penelope put her foot in the stirrup and swung up onto Midnight. She held a hand out to help Briar. Behind her, Briar leaned into her, spreading warmth and awareness through Pea's body. With a "snick-snick" of her tongue, Pea urged the horse into a trot, sending the now-awake beauty sliding farther forward. Her soft breasts pushed into Pea's back, and, smiling, they set off on the next leg of their adventure.

Chapter Six

Soon enough, they had to face the men Penelope had ditched in order to do the last part of the rescuing alone.

"Nice of you to return." Erik grabbed hold of Midnight's lead. His grip tightened on the leather, and his voice rose. "I wasn't sure what to think when you disappeared."

Once he said what he'd been holding in, Erik's anger seemed to have lost its wind, and he addressed Briar Rose.

"Miss, glad to have you join us." With a tip of his hat, he turned his attention back to Penelope. "Are ye both well enough to travel?"

"Good enough. We haven't been traveling for long today. We're ready," Pea directed.

A flurry of activity broke out at the encampment. Penelope kept catching the men stealing glances at the new princess.

"You are quite popular," Penelope said with a snicker. "I swear, Malcolm tripped over his bedroll three times already."

"If only I found their boorish jokes and

overbearing physicality attractive." With a sigh, Briar Rose leaned over Midnight's neck and stroked the gentle horse.

Once they started on the trail, nobody suggested stopping. With only a few stretching breaks, they pushed ahead. Finally, in the distance, Penelope spotted the castle.

"Ride ahead, young squire," Erik directed a lad. "Let them know of our arrival."

Torches illuminated the front of the castle as they approached. "It's gorgeous." The awe was evident in Briar's voice. "You live in a lovely home."

"Thank you. I hope you like staying here."

Pea got off the horse first and held out her hand to help Briar Rose. Her smooth hand made Pea want to hold on and never let go.

"Penelope!" A fiery bundle of energy launched herself into Pea's arms, separating her from Briar. "You're home!"

"Oh my Gwennie. I promised I would return." Tears sprang to Penelope's eyes. Hugging her sister felt like home. When she looked up, she noticed both of her brothers standing there, holding themselves back a bit.

"Oh, come here, too!"

She wrapped her arms around the three of them, feeling the love of her family surrounding her. While she'd enjoyed the adventure, the homecoming was even better.

"Ummm, I'd like you all to meet someone special." She broke free and wrapped her arm around Briar Rose's waist, guiding her in the middle.

"Are you Sleeping Beauty?" Gwennie asked, eyes wide.

With a gentle smile, Briar knelt, and tucked a wayward curl behind Gwennie's ear. "I suppose that's what some people might have called me, but I didn't always feel like I was sleeping."

Russell patted Penelope on the shoulder. "So you did it, eh, Sis? Rescued the fair maiden? Now what do you do with her?"

Fatigue hit Penelope hard, and her mind stuttered. "Ah, well."

"First, we offer both of these young women something warm to eat, a change of clothes, and plenty of time to rest." Her father stepped through the throng of well-wishers. "Welcome home, my daughter."

"I'm happy all's well." Penelope gave her dad a quick squeeze.

With her fingertips on the corners of her dress, Briar Rose curtseyed. "Your Highness. I thank you for the offer of hospitality."

"No need for formalities," he said. "I had good faith my daughter would succeed."

As the others walked toward the castle, Penelope took Gwennie's hand. "I've got your present."

"Ooooh." Her eyes widened in anticipation.

From her satchel, Penelope removed the bright pink rose. "This flower was wrapped around Princess Rose's bed."

Ahead, Briar stopped, watching their exchange with a wistful smile.

"Really?" Gwennie reached out, and touched the flower's stem. The moment it transferred from Penelope to her little sister, a glow radiated from the center, and in a flash, the petals turned white. "Wow, what happened?"

"I'm not sure. There was some sort of magic associated with it." Pea met the gaze of Briar Rose, and the other woman shrugged. "Or maybe you're magic."

"Well I love it. Thank you for thinking of me and for coming home safe."

The world of her worries dissipated, Gwennie bounced up, placed a kiss on Pea's cheek, and dashed off down the walkway.

Not too much had changed.

***

Being with Briar in the dream world was one thing. Now, in real life, reality came crashing back in. They returned to the kingdom to great fanfare, and the king sent word to Briar Rose's family. While Rose's parents traveled to their kingdom, she stayed in the castle. During the time she was in an enchanted sleep, they were awake but hadn't lived. It was like they were in their own stagnant suspended state.

Penelope's father still insisted upon the damn ball and her selection of a marriage partner. That meant a man from a neighboring royal family who would make a good match not just for her but the entire kingdom. *How can I put my wishes first and ignore the fate of everybody else?*

Every moment with Briar right now was like having a super-delicious dessert and totally gorging, only to never take another bite for the rest of her life. Penelope was going to have to give her up eventually. Did she want a lick of the illicit temptation, or would it be better to go without?

After a full day of making plans for the upcoming dance, they sat in the parlor of Briar Rose's room. The setting sun cast a warm glow, illuminating the rescued princess in a golden aura. She wore a frilly dress in sheer pink. Penelope alternated between fretting over the future and enjoying the moments they had together. She worried the silk of her dressing gown between her fingers until Rose reached over and stilled her hand.

"You know, if you were a gallant knight, about right now you'd be plundering the treasures?" Briar Rose said.

The teasing princess reclined against the velvet chaise lounge, her blonde tresses fanning out and cascading over her breasts. With a wink, she clasped the end of one tie on her bodice and slowly pulled it, until the collar scooped and exposed her ample cleavage.

Turmoil redoubled inside Penelope. She didn't quite know what to do being faced with the object of her desire returning favor.

"I'm lucky a knight didn't rescue you, or I would never have had my only adventure." Her response sounded flat to her ears.

A look of uncertainty passed over Briar's face, and she bunched up her robe, covering herself. "Since we've been back, you've shown no interest. Do you not want me like I thought you did?"

Ah, to talk of such issues. Penelope stood, pacing the room. She felt trapped. Confined within the walls of the castle. Her prison of expectations. Her bare feet slid on the cool marble floors. How dare she explain the problem?

"You see...." she began, only to stop and turn

around to stride back the other way. When she about-faced, Briar sat waiting, the same look—maybe a little less patient—upon her face.

"I see what? I see me making a fool of myself for you? I see me putting myself out there, and you having no interest? After all we shared in the dream-world and the glen, I thought I had read the situation. Wait, what situation? I thought I read *us* right."

"But you haven't lived," Penelope yelled, a bit too loud. She stopped, willing herself to calm down. She didn't want to draw unnecessary attention to their affairs. "You don't know what it's like, truly. The pressure. My father.... I can't see him accepting any of this."

Briar shifted her weight, tucking her legs under her body and letting that damn bodice fall open once again. As Penelope passed, Rose grabbed hold of her wrist and pulled her onto the lounge. She clutched both hands and met her eye to eye.

"I do understand. All too well. Haven't you figured out yet why no prince was able to wake me? No 'true love' to break the spell? I did not want any of them. Only you. Only you saw through all the obstacles to infuse me with life."

"When faced with no life whatsoever, the one you want becomes even more precious."

She leaned forward, bridging the invisible barrier between them. One wall built by Penelope, and the other erected by expectations forced upon her. The princess kissed her rescuer.

Silenced by love.

Over the years, Penelope had kissed a few would-be suitors. None of them had done it for her. Many were pleasant. But pleasant didn't take her very far.

She'd lain in bed, night after night, reliving the ho-hum moments with male suitors. She wanted spectacular. She longed to see stars bursting and feel the entire tingling body experience. Pretty high build-up for a kiss, especially after watching the glittery extravaganza of energy explode from Briar Rose.

They breathed in each other's air, lips to lips. Softly touching, waiting for the moment to shift from "Are we going to?" to "Ahh, pure bliss."

Penelope blinked, her view of Briar shadowed by her long lashes, and the princess returned into focus. The impact of seeing her fantasy in the flesh hit Penelope full force. Briar breached the last few inches. The once sleeping beauty parted her lips slightly, letting in Pea's tongue. A swirl of anticipation settled in her core, and something electric, magnetic passed between them. *Yes, that's it.*

With a moan, Penelope slipped her hand around Briar's waist, splaying out her fingers to touch, to claim more feeling. The pink chiffon bunched under her hand, and they seamed together, mouth to mouth.

As the fevered pace of their kiss increased, Briar reclined onto the chaise, taking Penelope with her until they lay side by side, facing each other. The princess slated soon to wed another grew dizzy from the sensation, the feeling of losing herself in the touch of another, and the short, quick breaths she took. They parted. Penelope focused on Briar's luscious mouth and the way her cheeks flushed red.

Pea ran her thumb along the other woman's lower lip and smiled. "That was nice."

"More than nice."

Once unleashed, Penelope desired more. She'd

waited this long to feel the object of her desire, fuck waiting any longer. She pressed her body into Briar's. When she looked down, she caught an eyeful of that magnificent cleavage. *Oh, how dare she tempt me so?*

With her teeth, she grabbed the closing strings and yanked them loose. She cupped those soft mounds from beneath, pushing them up and out of their confines. As soon as Briar's nipples hit the chilled air, they pebbled into hard nubs. Penelope brought her mouth against the precious strawberry pink. *Is everything on this woman rose-colored?*

***

Briar had pushed until her Sweet Pea couldn't take it anymore. Sometimes, she knew, others needed a little bit of incentive. After being trapped in the castle for so very long, she didn't want to wait any longer. The key would be to get her lover to feel the same way. How could the woman be so adventurous in dream land, cross multiple kingdoms, and face all those obstacles in order to save her, and then stagnate? She failed to understand the situation.

The men who'd tried to rescue her had failed hopelessly. Fortunately, Puss protected her virtue when some had attempted to have their way with her. Otherwise, she might have fallen long ago. Despite all the other attempts, only Penelope was able to break the magical bonds. That had to mean something. It was symbolic. Forget what society, or the king—her father—thought of her actions—and the result—spoke something else entirely.

The heat of their bodies infused the divide between them. Penelope moved to lie above her, pinning Briar. *Now that she has me in this position, what is she going to do? What do I want her to do?*

Everything.

Indecision nagged at her psyche. She vacillated between being subservient and going for what she wanted. In her heart, she knew, but, at the same time, she didn't want to scare Penelope away.

Penelope didn't need to make any sort of sacrifice to be with her. Once her parents came, and saw her alive and well, they'd bestow more than a fair number of gifts. She came with a dowry, and her brother certainly wasn't in the right condition to marry for position, sorry to say. Her kingdom was more progressive and inclusive than Penelope's. Love was love. The Fates had spoken. As her rescuer, Penelope automatically became the accepted mate. But, she didn't want to tell Pea her parents would support their union. It was wrong to hide the information, but she wanted Penelope to choose to be with her. Even though their marriage could be the political union both kingdoms needed, she wanted their relationship to be about passion and love. Was that too much to ask?

"Now it's you who seems to be off in a wonderland." Penelope ran her fingertips along the side of Briar's stomach.

"Just thinking about what your comment earlier. About the choices you have to make."

"Let's not get too serious right now," Penelope said. "I'm sorry to bring you down. Let's enjoy the time we have together because we don't know what tomorrow may bring."

But we could get serious, she wanted to scream. *We don't have to worry about tomorrow, or the day after, or even the year after that. We're two tough, independent women, and no matter the problems of our kingdoms, we can overcome them. Together.*

The words pushed to escape her lips, but she kept them closed tight. She refused to go there.

Instead, she pushed back physically.

"If you don't want me here, maybe I should leave." Without waiting for a response, Briar she broke the hold, and started halfheartedly collecting her meager belongings. She fought back tears. She couldn't be strong if she showed her weaknesses.

"What are you doing? What do you mean?" Penelope arrived at her side faster than she could imagine. She placed her hand over Briar's. "Stop. Please."

"I've already spent way too much of my life trapped. No happiness. No love. I don't want to waste any more time waiting."

Penelope brought her hands up to her face and pushed her hair back. She gave off a short growl of frustration. "I don't know how to do this. Why is this harder than I thought?"

"Just because you rescued the princess doesn't mean you get an automatic happily ever after," Briar said. "You need to work at it."

The ensuing quiet frightened her. Her heart pounded, and her throat constricted. What if this moment was it? If she left and returned to her kingdom, would she have to search for happiness all over? She'd formed a bond of love with Penelope. There had to be a reason she'd been the person—the right person—to break the sorceress's curse.

She grabbed hold of Penelope's hand and brought it against her chest. "Don't you understand?

I already chose you? And you chose me. There should be no decision to make. It's already been done."

The moment between them stretched out, as they stared into each other's eyes. Finally, Briar saw Pea relax her muscles. Briar wondered if maybe she had broken past some of the self-imposed boundaries around Penelope's heart. If their relationship had any chance of surviving, she needed to accept her choice of a female mate, before anyone else would. She would have to make those first steps.

This kiss that came next was unlike any other they'd shared. Rather than soft and gentle, Penelope tunneled her fingers into the back of Briar's hair and pulled her close. She stopped a breath apart, in challenge.

"Is this what you want?"

"Yes, oh, yes."

She looped her other arm around Briar's waist and tugged her tight against her body. Without all those bustles and slips, in their gowns, the press of Penelope's thighs through the material burned her with a refined passion. *Kiss me. Oh, kiss me.*

She didn't need to wish anymore. Lust fueled the kiss. Penelope claimed her lips, plunging her tongue into Briar's mouth. She sucked in a breath, only to be filled with sensuous pleasure.

Fuck tingling. Pure streaks of hot flashed through Briar's body, straight to her core, and the thought of taking Penelope into her bed and body caused her to grow wet between her legs. *Wanton.* She wanted this woman with everything she possessed.

Tearing her mouth from the other woman's, Briar pursed her lips, and breathed out. "Phhhh.

Wow. That was amazing."

Briar glanced downward, watching their chests flush red, the swell of them rising and falling. Penelope's darker nipples pressed through the thin material of her gown. Briar cupped one breast, rubbing her thumb over the point.

"My Rose. I don't know what to do with you. You push me away, and yet draw me ever closer," Penelope said, her voice a whisper. "I don't think I could ever grow tired of being with you."

"That's the whole point. You can't live without me. There is no choosing to be with me, or without me. We are."

Smack. Penelope lightly spanked Briar on the ass. "You are infuriating."

"Why? Because you want me? You might as well admit it." Briar squeezed her fingers together a bit more, pinching her would-be lover's nipple. "Admit it. Your body wants me. Your heart wants me. No matter what your head says."

"Oh, is that how you want to play it?" Penelope grabbed both of Briar's hands and brought them behind her back. The movement forced her breasts out, and those traitorous nipples of her own showed every bit of intention.

"Ooooh, unhand me," she fought against Penelope's hold. "You have no right."

"Don't I?" She arched an eyebrow, challenging Briar's protests. "I thought I rescued you. I saved your life. I basically brought you back from the dead. Moments ago, you said we didn't have a choice. Are you going back on that statement?"

"Pffft. No." Truth be told, it was difficult to stay haughty when placed in such a compromising position.

Penelope dipped her head down, tonguing Briar's nipples—first one and then the other—through the silky material. Oh the slow pace was maddeningly erotic. The extra texture added another level of pleasure, and yet she wanted Penelope's mouth against her skin.

"Do you perhaps need a lesson in manners?" Penelope asked. "If we're going to have any type of relationship, we're going to have to set some ground rules. And the first will probably be not to tease me."

"Tease you? You're the one who keeps running hot and cold. What am I supposed to do? Sit around and wait for you to decide what you want to do with me?"

"If you really don't like me taking control, I think we can test the theory out pretty easily." Penelope held Briar's hands together with one hand, and with the other palmed her thigh. "What does your body say?"

The truth would be learned easily enough. Her body loved the attention. The battle between their wills only amped the intensity. Just because she wanted to be with a woman—this woman—didn't mean she didn't want to feel the intensity of being taken, being dominated. She needed someone equally strong, and even more so.

With precision, Penelope inched up the hem of Briar's gown. Since the fabric almost touched the floor, the trip was a long one. Her fingers crawled over the material, bunching it up, and traveling higher and higher. The now fully awake princess's breath caught with each caress. Penelope watched her intently, as if she dared Briar Rose to ask her to stop.

Briar's face flushed, knowing what Penelope was about to find between her legs—pure evidence of her continued attraction. She hadn't been hiding her desire. She'd been asking for more. Confirmation of their union.

A breeze drifted over her upper thighs and the material rose even further, until the apex of her legs lay exposed. "Well look at those pretty pink lace panties," Penelope said. "I'm ready to peel open those petals."

Her deft fingers brushed over Briar's nether lips, and another shot of pleasure went through her body. Penelope leaned into the other woman, arching her hips.

"Oh, yes, look at that. So wet, and is all of this for me?"

She gritted her teeth, and shut her eyes. *She damn well knows the effect she has on my body.* They'd walked down that path before in the dream-world. She wanted Penelope to admit what lay in her heart.

"What? Are you not going to answer me now?" Penelope asked. "What's the matter, cat got your tongue?"

"Low blow."

Her laugh—rich, dark, and full of the wonderment of life—filled the bedchamber. "I didn't mean it that way. I wasn't referencing your brother. Now tell me. Why are you being so difficult?"

Silence. She couldn't ask for love. It had to be given freely.

"And there you go again. Retreating to whatever magic castle you have in your head. I may have rescued you from that tower, but you still need to free your mind."

Penelope dropped Briar's gown and released her arms. Instantaneous relief, and yet a sense of loss, of missed opportunities washed over Briar.

They'd come so far, and yet the journey was not yet over.

"And on that note, I think it's time I bid you good night," Penelope said. "Tomorrow is another day."

Once the door slammed behind her, Briar sank into the bed. The light of the candle cast flickering shadows against the wall, and she pondered Penelope's parting words. She cast blame on Penelope for wanting to make the best choice to preserve her family and kingdom, and yet she continued to hold back. After being trapped once, fear held her heart in check.

Chapter Seven

D ust from the trail billowed in a cloud, fast approaching. Hope mixed with joy blossomed in Briar Rose's chest. She clenched her hands, willing them to stop shaking.

"I think they're here." She peered out the window, waiting for a glimpse to confirm her beliefs.

Despite their argument the night before, Penelope stood by her side, her hand on the small of her back. "Are you sure?"

"Look, there it is!" She pointed out the window. A glint of gold sparkled in the sunlight. "That's the family crest, on our carriage."

The carriage followed the path toward the heart of the castle. As it neared, Briar Rose lifted the hem of her dress and took off down the hall to the staircase.

"Puss. Here, Puss," she called, as she ran. "It's Mom and Dad."

Her voice carried through the castle, luring out her wayward brother.

Meow.

She scooped him up along the way, and cradled

him like a child.

"Can you believe it? We get to see Mom again after all these years."

Raw-er.

"Oh don't be such a pussycat," she said. "I'm sure they'll be happy to see you, too."

"Wait up, wait up," called Penelope, following close behind.

The last time they'd seen Puss, her parents hadn't been too pleased. They blamed him for the confrontation with the sorceress. He'd screwed her over in a failed relationship. The sorceress took her misery out on everyone else in an extreme way—if she couldn't have love, nobody would. She'd turned him into a low-level feline and placed the spell on Briar Rose.

Outside the castle, the staff had trimmed all the bushes and pruned the flowers. The castle looked fairy-tale-like with its high turrets and sparkling arches. For the impending ball, the king had ordered pink chiffon wrapped around the tree trunks and oversized bows hung from the windows.

Small rocks shot out from under the wheels of the carriage as it sped along the path, and the moment it stopped, the door sprang open.

Briar Rose's father stepped out and assisted his wife.

"Daddy," Briar yelled. As he turned, she launched into his arms.

He smoothed her hair. "Oh, my girl. I thought I was never going to see you again."

Briar's mother stood on the carriage steps, tears glistening in her eyes. Penelope stood back, feeling disconnected from the scene before her. Keeping one arm around his long-lost daughter, the visiting king extended his other hand toward his wife. She gracefully came down the steps, only to wrap her arms around Briar.

Rawr. Me-owww. Puss circled in and out of the mother's ankles, making a terrible racket.

Finally, she released Briar and picked up the almost-yodeling cat. Penelope had never seen him act so distressed.

"Oh honey." The mother pressed her face into his soft fur. "The spell on your brother didn't break at the same time as yours, and ours?"

"I'm sorry, Mum." Briar cast her gaze onto the ground. "I'm not sure what it'll take. Maybe Penelope has an idea. Pea? She's the one who rescued me."

All turned their attention to her, and a flush spread up Penelope's chest and face. "Well," she hesitated for more time. "If it's not something external that's kept him in this state, then it might be something internal."

The king moved forward, encompassing her in an awkward hug. "Thank you for saving our daughter."

"If you don't mind"—The queen took a low bow— "what were you saying about Puss?"

"It's just Briar Rose shared a little about how he came to be in this state. After he broke off relations with the sorceress. Maybe it's not something we can do in order to break the spell, but something he needs to do, or change."

"Interesting," the king said.

The cat's golden eyes regarded her, and she looked away first. "Now, I'm sure you're all tired from a long journey," Penelope said. "Why don't you come in and rest for a spell. We have plenty of refreshments."

The travelers' jovial spirits spread through the castle, and all of Penelope's siblings dropped in for a visit. Gwennie was particularly besotted with the queen. Watching the two together made her heart pang for the loss of their maternal figure. Gwennie had never known the unconditional love of a mother like the one who had sacrificed her life in order to give Gwennie hers.

After refreshments, Penelope left the visitors in their quarters and dressed for the evening. The seamstress had created a lush dress spun in gold that would shimmer in even the darkest night. Arms outstretched, Penelope waited for her attendants to drape the gown over her head. The material floated around her with a *hush*, as if silencing all her desires.

"Ready, ma'am?"

"Yes, it's time." She sucked in a breath as the woman yanked the back strings, drawing her waist into an impossible size. There'd be no eating of the grand buffet this evening.

Next, she moved to the vanity, barely sitting on the edge of the seat, as another woman coiffed her hair. She closed her eyes, not wanting to see the transformation in progress. Each step took her further from the person she was. Finally, she gazed in the mirror at a queen-in-waiting she didn't recognize.

She was ready.

***

Music swirled around her, and Penelope tried to squash the sense of being trapped. Tonight, her father wanted her to choose a mate. Her dress felt too tight. Her smile felt even tighter. Then she caught sight of Briar Rose. She wore lavender, and looked even more ravishing than she did in pink. She sat with her parents, watching all the activities. As if she could feel Penelope's gaze, she raised her eyes.

Coming to a stop before them, Penelope wasn't quite sure of her intentions. Until the moment came.

"Sir. Madam. I expect your quarters suit you?"

"Oh, you have a lovely home," the queen said. "Thank you again for everything you've done."

Embarrassment caused her face to heat. "It was nothing, really."

"Tsk-tsk," the visiting king corrected. "No modesty needed. There were many a lad we hired for the task. None succeeded, and few even returned."

"Well, it was my pleasure," she said. "Would you mind if I asked Briar Rose to dance? I realize it's not traditional, but...."

The queen batted her hand to stop Penelope from talking. "Say no more."

Her heart stuttered. *What have I done? Briar's mother is going to tell me off.*

"You two have formed a special bond. Tradition can kiss my stately arse."

"Mother," the king exclaimed. "You can see where our daughter gets her feisty nature. We mustn't keep you any longer." He gestured to them to run off, like children going for a tumble in the yard.

Penelope turned toward Briar Rose and held out her hand. "M'lady, would you do me the honor?"

"I'd love to dance with you. It's what I've been waiting for."

Dancing with another woman, in all their

accruements, was easier imagined than done. Unlike the exchange in their nightgowns, layers upon layers of fabric and lace separated them.

Briar laughed as they fought to press closer, and to wrap their hands around the other's waist. "Didn't think this one through very much, did we?"

"If we do this again, one of us must wear a less fluffy dress," Penelope said in all seriousness.

The moment they gained position, the clamor around the dance floor floated away, and they twirled and whirled, ease and freedom guiding each footstep.

Rose's soft breasts tempted Penelope as they danced. In her dreams, she'd lavished and ravished the other woman, but she longed to truly touch her and taste her in real life. Pea gazed at the creamy curves of her cleavage, which enticed her to run away from the ball, and escape to their own pleasures in bed.

But duty called. The night was still young.

"Soon enough," Rose said, her voice a melodious balm.

Penelope raised her eyes to meet Rose's. "For what?"

The lightest brush against the top of her bottom made Penelope jump a bit higher on the next step. "Oooh."

A devilish smile spread across Rose's face. "For us to be alone, and for me to make you mine."

This time, Penelope didn't mistake the purposeful movement of Rose angling her slender hands down, so her fingertips pressed into Pea's ass. Despite all the layers between them, she imagined every stroke. A flush of desire spread through her body. She'd never thought she'd meet someone who felt the same way about her. One who she shared so much in common with.

The tempo of the song wound down, and the dancers on the floor stopped, the swirling rainbow of dresses slowing. Those in attendance clapped.

Her father, the king, stood from his throne, and a page blew his trumpet to get everyone's attention. The band grew quieter and quieter, tapering the volume. The king cleared his throat and spread his arms toward the crowd. Penelope looked up, her chest tightening, not sure what was going to come from her father's mouth. He might not be pleased with her actions, but she hoped someday he'd come to understand her reasons. Beside her, Rose slipped her hand into Pea's and squeezed.

"No matter what," she whispered, "I'm here."

"Thank you all for joining me and our royal family on this wondrous occasion."

More applause. But of course they had to clap, no matter what he said.

"As you know, tonight, my beautiful daughter was to choose a mate to rule by her side into the future."

A murmur of anticipation broke out in a wave among the dancers, and those surrounding Penelope and her partner moved backward, creating a circle around them.

Rose's lavender dress shimmered with a silver overlay that twinkled with each graceful movement. Rose dropped Penelope's hand and bowed. She gave one nod of her head with a slight smile and stepped aside. While mere inches now separated them, the divide and expectations between them felt insurmountable.

No matter where she looked, everyone watched her. Several of the princes and knights in attendance caught her eye with a knowing look. Their expressions seemed to convey their confidence. She had to pick one of them, right? Each suitor would imagine himself a proper candidate.

"This ball was not my daughter's idea, but my own. And not in my formal capacity as king, but as an interfering father who only wants the best for his child."

At those words, Penelope turned back toward her father, focusing all her attention upon him. His tone was changing in a way she rarely heard. Beside him stood her eldest brother who nodded toward her.

"It is not up to me to say who she must make a union with, just as it is not up to me to decide when the right time is. I thank all who came out tonight. You will not be forgotten. Instead, let's celebrate her brave rescue of the Princess Briar Rose, and their fortuitous budding friendship. I welcome Princess Rose's parents as my new allies."

He lifted a gold chalice and turned toward Rose's parents, who sat alongside him. In turn, they lifted their own glasses of wine.

"Here, here."

"Cheers."

As he raised the glass to his lips, he met Penelope's gaze, and she mouthed "thank you." He acknowledged her with a tilt of his head. After he sipped fully, toasting to his daughter, he set down the glass and clapped his hands once again.

"The night is still young. Drink up, and keep dancing." He twirled his finger in a circle. At that moment, Penelope saw something she never thought she'd see in her lifetime. The king gave a longing glance at Rose's aunt—a younger sister to the queen who had come for the evening. The maiden curtsied and her face flushed red at the king's acknowledgement.

Perhaps, there was hope for a love match of his own. The thought made her even happier.

A prince as handsome as the rest of them stepped in her line of sight and held out his hand. She didn't remember his name. The princes all ran together. "Do you mind if I have this dance?" he asked.

A well of panic flared. It would be rude to say no and turn him away. But with freedom before her, she didn't want to go backward.

"Oh, I'm sorry. I'm feeling a bit woozy." Rose swayed and leaned against Penelope, giving her a quick wink of conspiracy. Her soft voice lilted higher. "Would you two mind helping me over to one of those chairs?"

"It would be my pleasure and my duty," the prince said, sliding his arm around her waist.

"Pea, you must come sit and watch over me while I rest." She laid it on thick.

Once safely ensconced in a velvet high-backed chair, Rose waved over a distant cousin—a rare, ripe beauty of eighteen just making her debut.

"Lily, do me a favor, please, and dance with this kind gentleman."

He couldn't refuse. He clasped his hands behind his lower back, elbows out, and bent at the waist in a bow toward Penelope. "Your Highness, if you will excuse me."

"Oh please do," she gestured toward the dance

floor. "I think I twisted my ankle in that last go round. I wouldn't be too much fun anyway."

Lily took the prince's offered arm, and they swiftly joined the twirling silks on the dance floor.

"You are a crafty one," Penelope said.

Rose rested the back of her hand over her forehead, and swooned. "Do tell, are you saying I was faking it?"

She leaned in closer. "All of it."

"You should have seen the look of horror on your face when he asked you to dance. You need to learn to deflect, and a little diplomacy wouldn't hurt. But that was a nice addition about twisting your ankle. You're lucky, though, he didn't get down on his knees to inspect under your gown."

The last words she punctuated boldly.

"Briar Rose!"

"What? You know that's where I want to be."

Her lovely mate blushed the sweetest, most innocent color pink, but by now Penelope knew her much better. "Do you think we could escape to somewhere more private?" Briar Rose asked. She worried her lower lip, and Penelope wanted to do the biting.

Rather than running away, Penelope led Briar to the king's table, and placed a kiss on his cheek. "Thank you, Father, for letting me be me."

"All I've ever wanted was for you to be happy." He nodded at Briar. "And this lass seems to do that."

"Would you mind if we stepped out? We have a lot to discuss."

"I was young once, too. I understand the call of

budding love. Don't spend too much time talking." The king winked at them. "We'll work things out another day."

They bid good night to Rose's parents, and dashed to Penelope's sleeping quarters.

"Now, what was I saying about being under your gown?" Briar teased, lifting at the hem of her chosen's dress.

Penelope pushed her hands away. "We've spent too much time in all matters of being half-dressed. I want to do this right, and I want to be with you. Turn around."

With deft fingers, Pea loosened the back of Briar Rose's garment. Still, it wasn't fast enough. Her heart thudded in her chest, threatening to race into overdrive.

"That should do the trick," Penelope said. "Now, step out."

Briar Rose stood before her lover in bloomers of pale pink with delicate roses—rosebuds—along the trim, and her chemise.

"You are so very lovely," Penelope said.

"Thank you. Now, your turn."

Pea quickly stripped her layers off, until nothing remained between them except the barest of coverings.

In unison, they walked toward the bed, with Pea reaching to remove the thick velvet coverlet. Briar ran her palm along the texture and climbed the ladder to the mattress.

"What's with all this fuss?" she asked. "It's a bit suffocating."

"Do you think?"

The pillows and throws and ruffles dwarfed Pea.

Rose got on her knees and tossed off rounded pillows and long skinny ones and heavy cloying comforters that would provide claustrophobia and little comfort. In minutes, the top was bare.

"Are you sure?" Penelope wrung her hands. "I was always told...."

"And how is that working out for you? Not very well by the purple marks beneath your lovely eyes and those pills you keep popping. Now, shut up and let me love you."

"Love me?" Penelope slipped across the sheet, bringing Rose close until they lay breast to breast, facing each other. "Do you love me?"

Now isn't the time to be proud or fearful. If I ever am going to bare my heart, this is it.

"I love you with all of my being, and then more. Heaps and heaps! Taller than all those blasted covers I threw on the ground," Rose said. "Think of a tiny pea covered in a stack of mattresses and pillows and blankets. I love you more than all of that combined."

Briar Rose waited. Pea blinked. A tear slid down her cheek. "I never thought." Penelope's voice hitched. "Somebody like you could love me. I love you."

"Don't cry." Briar Rose kissed away the wetness, trailing a line across her chin before settling on her lips. Pressing her fingers between Penelope's legs, Rose sought the heat. "Time to take off the rest of these clothes."

"Oh, yes."

Passion waiting, they fumbled, all sense of propriety gone. Briar closed her mouth over Penelope's breasts, teasing the nipples until they rose in stiff peaks. She sighed into the welcoming softness and rubbed her fingers on her lover's clit.

"Mmmm. I want to feel you on me, against me," she said. "We'll have plenty of time to explore each other later. Now, I need you."

Briar Rose shifted to mount Penelope, bracing her elbows on either side. Breasts smashed against breasts, stomach against stomach and, if they angled their hips in just the right manner, pussy to pussy. Beneath her, Pea ground her pelvis upward, rubbing and rubbing in the right spot. She reached her slender hand between their bodies to plunge two fingers into Briar's wet channel.

Her moan got lost in the next kiss, until she found her voice. "Oh-oh-oh," Rose exclaimed. "My love."

With a last kiss, Briar Rose moved below the covers. "It's your turn."

She sought her prize with her nose, tunneling into the rich scent. She flicked the tip of her tongue against the engorged nub and Penelope tightened the muscles in her thighs. Alternating between fingering, licking, nibbling, and sucking, Briar feasted on her lover. She infused all the love she felt into making love. The joy of finding her mate flowed through her psyche, and she connected on a higher level with Penelope. As the magic of their union brought them closer together physically, Briar Rose increased the friction— faster and faster. Penelope's hips rose off the bed and her entire body pulled taut.

"Yes, yes, yes." Shudders surfed her limbs, and then she lay limp. "Come here." She lifted the bedspread.

"Feel better?"

"If you only knew." Sleepily, Penelope embraced

Briar. "You are my Princess-So-Charming. Will you spend eternity with me, ruling our kingdoms?"

"There's nothing I'd like more."

And the princess who once could never wake anticipated the future, while gazing at the slumbering beauty in her arms.

If anyone is wondering what happened to good ol' Puss.... Will he become human again, and find his true love? Well, that's a tale for another day.

About the Author

A Southern California native, Louisa Bacio can't imagine living far away from the ocean. The multi-published author of erotic romance enjoys writing within all realms – from short stories to full-length novels.

Bacio shares her household with a supportive husband, two daughters growing "too fast," and a multitude pet craziness: Two dogs, five fish tanks, an aviary, hamsters, rabbits and hermit crabs. In her other life, she teaches college classes in English, journalism and popular culture.

Check out the latest happenings via her blog http://louisabacio.blogspot.com

Other Books by Louisa Bacio